ABT

P9-BIY-555

A NOTE TO PARENTS

Early Step into Reading Books are designed for preschoolers and kindergartners who are just getting ready to read. The words are easy, the type is big, and the stories are packed with rhyme, rhythm, and repetition.

We suggest that you read this book to your child the first few times, pointing to each word as you go. Soon your child will start saying the words with you. And before long, he or she will try to read the story alone. Don't be surprised if your child uses the pictures to figure out the text—that's what they're there for! The important thing is to develop your child's confidence—and to show your child that reading is fun.

When your child is ready to move on, try the rest of the steps in our Step into Reading series. **Step 1 Books** (preschool–grade 1) feature the same easy-to-read type as the Early Step into Reading Books, but with more words per page. **Step 2 Books** (grades 1–3) are both longer and slightly more difficult, while **Step 3 Books** (grades 2–3) introduce readers to paragraphs and fully developed plot lines. **Step 4 Books** (grades 2–4) offer exciting nonfiction for the increasingly independent reader.

The grade levels assigned to the five steps are intended only as guides. Some children move through all five steps very rapidly; others climb the steps over a period of several years. Either way, these books will help your child "step into reading" in style!

For my parents, Michael and Beverly Corey,
and their boating friends in Myrtle Beach, South Carolina
—S.C.

For Jane, Alex, and Joe
—M.R.

Text copyright © 2001 by Shana Corey. Illustrations copyright © 2001 by Mike Reed.
All rights reserved under International and Pan-American Copyright Conventions. Published
in the United States by Random House, Inc., New York, and simultaneously in Canada by
Random House of Canada Limited, Toronto.

www.randomhouse.com/kids

Library of Congress Cataloging-in-Publication Data
Corey, Shana.
Boats! / by Shana Corey ; illustrated by Mike Reed.
p.   cm. — (Early step into reading)
SUMMARY: Illustrations and simple rhyming text present all kinds of boats—yachts, toy boats,
tugs, ferryboats, and more.
ISBN 0-375-80221-5 (trade) — ISBN 0-375-90221-X (lib. bdg.)
[1. Boats and boating—Fiction. 2. Stories in rhyme.] I. Reed, Mike, 1951– ill. II. Title.
III. Series.
PZ8.3.C8183 Bo 2001
[E]—dc21   00-044533

Printed in the United States of America   April 2001   10 9 8 7 6 5 4 3 2 1

STEP INTO READING, RANDOM HOUSE, and the Random House colophon are registered trademarks
and EARLY STEP INTO READING and colophon are trademarks of Random House, Inc.

Early Step into Reading™

Boats!

by Shana Corey
illustrated by Mike Reed

Random House 🏠 New York

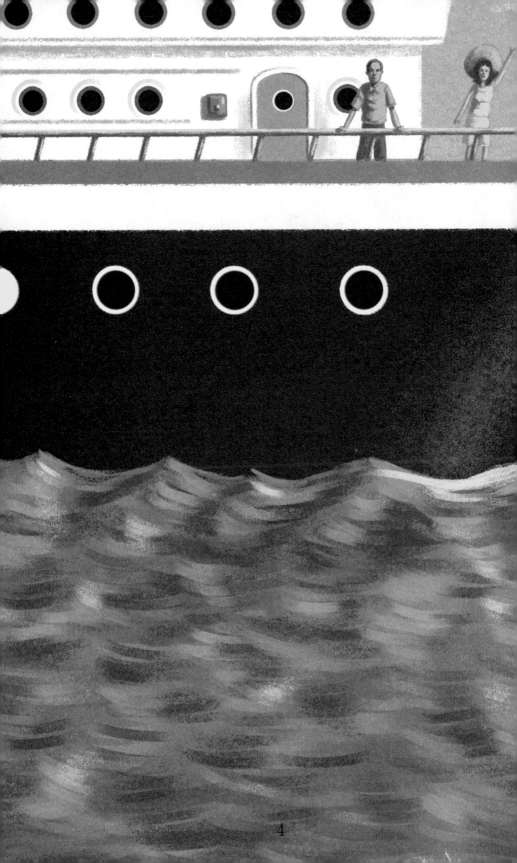

Big boat.

Little boat.

Float, float, float.

Fancy boat.

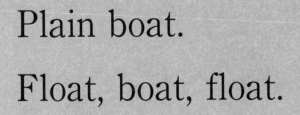

Plain boat.

Float, boat, float.

Boat in the bathtub.

Boat on the sea.

Boat to carry Duckie.

Boat to carry me!

Ferryboat.

Houseboat.

Chug, chug, chug.

Motorboat.

Tugboat.

Lug, lug, lug.

Boat packed with people.

Boat just for one.

Busy, busy working boat.

Boat just for fun.

Old boat.

New boat.

High boat.

Low.

Boat by itself.

Boats in a row.

Sailboat.

Showboat.

Fast boat.

Boats, boats,
and more boats!

Go, boats!
Go!